cock-a-doodle-hooooooo!

For Kristina Granström, with love
– MM & BG

ISBN-13: 978-0-545-11604-6
ISBN-10: 0-545-11604-X

12 11 10 9 8 7 6 5 4 3 2 1 8 9 10 11 12 13/0

Printed in the U.S.A. 40

First Scholastic printing, October 2008

cock-a-doodle-hooooooo!

Mick Manning   Brita Granström

SCHOLASTIC INC.
New York Toronto London Auckland Sydney
Mexico City New Delhi Hong Kong Buenos Aires

One stormy night, an owl walked into a farmyard. He was cold, lost and lonely, with no place to go, so he squeezed through a hole in a shed.

It was warm and cozy in there, and he fell fast asleep.

In the morning Owl woke to a nip and a pinch. He heard clucking and squawking. He was surrounded by bony feet and beady eyes.

He was in a hen house . . . .

He's no hen!
He's no rooster!
We need a rooster!

HOO?
What
a shame!
We could
give him a
try.

"Can he peck like a rooster?"
said one bossy hen.
Owl tried to peck.

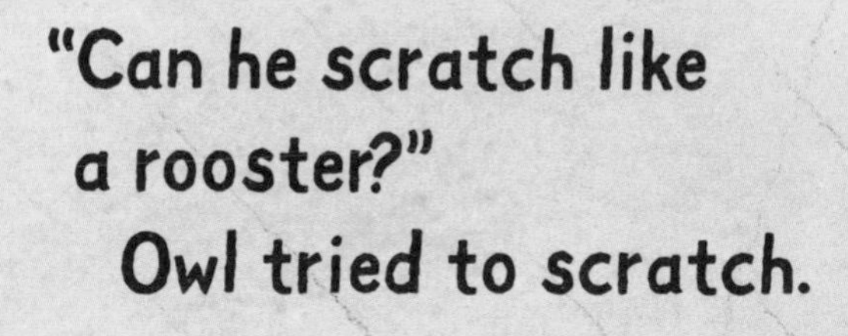

"Can he scratch like
a rooster?"
Owl tried to scratch.

"Can he cock-a-doodle
like a rooster?"
Owl tried a cock-a-doodle.

HOOO!

The hens awarded him
NO POINTS
for pecking.

NO POINTS
for scratching.

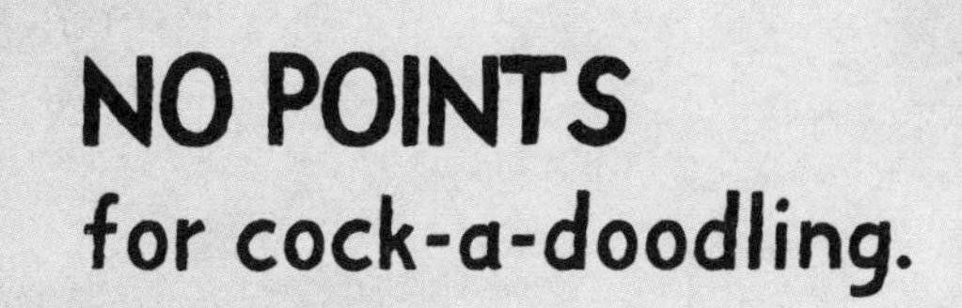

NO POINTS
for cock-a-doodling.

What a clown!
What a loser!

"Hoo-hoo!" cried Owl sadly. He liked the warm, cozy hen house and the yard dappled with spring sunshine.

The speckled hen put her bony wings around him.

"I'll teach you how to be a rooster!" she clucked . . .

... and she did.
Owl learned how to ...

march up and down,

guard the hen house

and puff out his feathers!
He was doing very well . . .

. . . until the other hens said, "Try and cock-a-doodle!"

Owl tried very hard. He tried his best . . .
but he was an owl after all,
and he just hooted like an owl.

HOOO!

The other hens were not impressed.
Goggle eyes!
A rooster MUST cock-a-doodle!
All he does is hoot!
What sort of an egg did you hatch out of – a square one?

Owl got cross. He'd had enough.
He was hungry and he was fed up
with the silly hens. So he said,

"I'm an owl, not a fowl!

Owls aren't hens.

We hoot in the moonlight.

We don't peck corn,

we catch . . . we catch . . . ."

"Rats!"

squawked a hen, peering into the hen house.

A rat!
A rat is in our
hen house!

The rat was stealing eggs,
eating corn, chasing chicks!

When Owl heard this,
he pricked up his ear tufts.
He flexed his sharp claws
and stretched his soft wings.
Then, silently as a floating
feather, he flew across
the hen house . . . .

Snip! Snap!

He caught the rat and gobbled it up. The rat was tasty and delicious. The hens were speechless!

They fussed around Owl in a flurry of feathers and clucks....

And Owl puffed out his chest with
a swagger and shouted,
"COCK-A-DOODLE-HOOOO!"
Our very own
special rooster!
Our beautiful
goggle-eyed
rooster!

Our hero!
Our rat-catching owl!